To Dominic

moo
went the cow

by Hatman

Illustrated by Lydia Farahat

Enjoy
Hatman

Written by Martyn J. G. Ware
Book illustrations by Lydia Farahat www.lydiagracestudios.com

To my Mother Hazel Ware,
for giving me wings so I
could fly.

as she chewed on her very crunchy chow.

to eat

Moo went the cow,

as the tractor drove by
with the plough.

as she slurped water from the trough.

drink

Moo went the cow,

as she did a big let off.

toilet

Moo went the cow,

as the combine
harvester did mow.

cut

as the farmer milked her udders.

milk

Moo went the cow,

as the wind blew she shudders.

Moo went the cow,

as she was very very sleepy.

About the Author

Hatman is a poet and educator with over 30 years experience working with young people. He has featured in various magazines and on BBC radio. He now brings his writing to life in the form of children's picture books.

Hatman uses a mix of poetry and sign language to convey his stories to a younger audience. He was inspired by fatherhood to start writing children books and was influenced by his mother who was a Special Needs Inclusion practitioner.

To find out more about #Hatman and his latest work visit www.hatman.co.uk

About the Illustrator

Lydia Farahat is a free-lance illustrator and arts, health & wellbeing practitioner. She illustrates children's books, commissions and animated productions.

Lydia also runs a variety of art workshops for children, women and vulnerable people, as she has a passion for helping others develop their creativity.

You can find her work on www.lydiagracestudios.com or follow along with her tutorials on www.youtube.com/c/LydiaGraceStudios

Printed in Great Britain
by Amazon